ESCAPE
FROM EARTH

Janice Greene

PAGETURNERS

SUSPENSE

Boneyard
The Cold, Cold Shoulder
The Girl Who Had Everything
Hamlet's Trap
Roses Red as Blood

ADVENTURE

A Horse Called Courage
Planet Doom
The Terrible Orchid Sky
Up Rattler Mountain
Who Has Seen the Beast?

MYSTERY

The Hunter
Once Upon a Crime
Whatever Happened to
  Megan Marie?
When Sleeping Dogs Awaken
Where's Dudley?

DETECTIVE

The Case of the Bad Seed
The Case of the Cursed Chalet
The Case of the Dead Duck
The Case of the Wanted Man
The Case of the Watery Grave

SCIENCE FICTION

Bugged!
Escape from Earth
Flashback
Murray's Nightmare
Under Siege

SPY

A Deadly Game
An Eye for an Eye
I Spy, e-Spy
Scavenger Hunt
Tuesday Raven

SADDLEBACK
EDUCATIONAL PUBLISHING
www.sdlback.com

ISBN-13: 978-1-56254-131-6
ISBN-10: 1-56254-131-5
eBook: 978-1-60291-233-5

Printed in the United States of America

18 17 16 15 14   4 5 6 7 8

CONTENTS

Chapter 1 5

Chapter 2 14

Chapter 3 22

Chapter 4 31

Chapter 5 39

Chapter 6 49

Chapter 7 57

Chapter 8 64

Chapter 9 71

Chapter 1

I take pride in the fact that I'm smart about people. You know what I mean? I can tell right away if someone's going to be nice or boring or dumb. Take my father, for instance. Just one look at his droopy eyes and mouth tells you that the guy's a loser, a quitter. I could have told my mom from the beginning that he'd never stick around.

So when I first met my roommate, Darryl, I was really disappointed. He had beady little eyes and a tight mouth. *Self-centered and sneaky*, I thought to myself. *Probably a weirdo*. But that wasn't even half the story!

He stood at the door of our dorm room, holding two suitcases and an unusually wide briefcase.

"Here, let me give you a hand," I said, reaching for the briefcase.

"No!" he almost screamed.

"Okay, okay!" I backed off.

He brought in the two suitcases. "My name is Darryl," he said.

"I'm Nick," I said. I reached out to shake his hand, but he just gave me a long look. "I'm glad to be with you. You are a safe person," he finally added.

"A *safe* person?" I thought to myself. "How odd."

"Where are you from?" I asked.

"Kazakhstan," he said.

"No kidding? You're sure a long way from home," I said. "Is your name really Darryl?"

"My real name you wouldn't be able to pronounce," he said. He looked at me hopefully. "I hope we'll like San Francisco State," he added.

I'd like it a lot more with another roommate, I thought.

Later, I asked him if he wanted to go

down to the dining hall. "Always give people a chance," my mom is forever saying, but Darryl said he wasn't hungry. That was fine with me. At lunch I'd met a friendly guy named Mike. Maybe I'd run into him. He's studying computer animation, same as me.

Maybe it was the second helping of greasy fries, but I had a weird dream that night. I dreamed that Darryl had this strange contraption, a tangle of wires and tubes. He was speaking into it—babbling on and on in some strange language. That can't be how they talk in Kazakhstan, I thought.

The next morning, Darryl was gone before I woke up. He must have had an early class. I was thinking how nice it was to have the place to myself when there was a loud knock on the door. It was a girl. The first thing that caught my eye was her legs, which were really tan. She had a wide forehead, which I always associate with honest people. Her eyes were a deep, warm brown. I knew she was someone special.

"I'm Kara," she said, shaking my hand energetically. "I'm from the dorm across the way. Would you mind if I came in and leaned out your window for just a few minutes?"

"The window?" I asked in confusion. "Well, okay, come on in."

She had a canvas bag full of tools. "I'm just going to drill a little hole in the wall of the building outside your window. Is that okay? I'm setting up a clothesline," she said.

"They *let* you do that?" I asked.

"You'd better believe I had to talk them into it," she chuckled.

"You're not from around here, are you?" I asked.

"No, I'm not. I'm from Arizona," she said. "Why?"

"That explains your nice tan—plus the fact that you're totally insane," I laughed. "I can't imagine putting up a clothesline in the foggiest city in the country! It'll take your clothes a *month* to dry! But what the heck. It's got to be a great idea, anyway."

"Oh, and why is that?" she said, giving me a sassy look.

"Otherwise you never would have knocked on my door. In fact, I think you ought to reel in your clothes from my room—so you can come visit me every time you do your wash."

"Well, you work pretty fast!" she said with a smile. She had a great smile.

I helped her mount the clothesline reel outside the window. "Now, how are you going to get the line from one building to the other?" I asked.

"I was hoping I could throw it from my window to your window," she said.

"Have you got a good arm? It's three stories down if you miss," I said.

"I won't miss," she said confidently. "And I'll get really mad if *you* miss."

The buildings were about 15 feet

apart. Just a few minutes after Kara left, I saw her open her window and wave. "Ready?" she called out.

"Ready!" I yelled. The ball of cord arched through the air and sailed into my open window. In fact, it landed hard and heavy—right in my hands. "Perfect!" I called out to her.

"Of course!" she answered.

Kara attached the cord to the reel at her end. She walked back into my room as I finished attaching my end.

"Now, *that's* a clothesline!" I said. "Say, Kara, I have coffee and a bag of cookies here. Let's celebrate."

"Don't you have some studying to do?" Kara asked with a teasing grin.

"Well, sure," I said. "But it can wait. Tell me about yourself. I don't even know what classes you're taking, what kind of movies you like, why you came all the way to San Francisco—or whether you like mint chocolate cookies or vanilla wafers."

"Both," she said, laughing.

At that moment, Darryl came in.

When he saw Kara there, he looked alarmed. He turned to me and said in a low voice, "She must leave here. She is not a safe person."

"Are you out of your skull?" I said.

"*Excuse me?*" said Kara, giving Darryl a hard, questioning look.

"Please!" Darryl insisted. He looked like he was about to panic.

"Take it easy, buddy. Maybe you're the one who needs to leave!" I said.

What a dork! I was going to grab him and hustle him out the door. But when I reached for his shoulders, a shock ran through my fingers and up my arms. "Ow!" I yelled.

"What? What'd he do?" said Kara.

Darryl gave me a pitiful, pleading look. In a few moments, the pain had faded from my hands and arms. I stared at him, wondering if I'd imagined the shock. Finally, I said to Kara, "Let's get out of here."

We had coffee in her room. "Why did you let that guy Darryl push you around?" Kara wanted to know.

"I guess I felt sorry for him," I said.

"You need to get rid of him," Kara grumbled. "He's unstable."

"Maybe I should give him a chance," I said. "I don't really know him yet."

She leaned close to me, her eyebrows raised. "*Nick!* Don't wait until he does something terrible," she said.

"Maybe you're right," I said.

By the time I got back to my room, I was ready to call the head of student housing. There was still plenty of time to ask for a new roommate. But Darryl seemed to be reading my mind. I hadn't been there for five minutes when he begged me to let him stay.

He said, "I'm sorry to make you miserable, but please let me keep my place. I will have to be leaving soon, anyway."

He looked so anxious and sad that I

felt myself giving in. "Really?" I said.

"I have family difficulties," he said quietly. He stood up and grabbed his briefcase. "I'll see you later," he added.

I had the place to myself all morning. In fact, the whole floor of the dorm seemed empty—which was nice for a change. I called Kara and asked her to come with me to a movie tomorrow. What luck to meet such a cool girl! I wanted to see her as often as possible. I was just getting to my homework when there was a sharp knock on the door.

It was two serious-looking guys in business suits. They looked like brothers. "Campus Security," the taller one said. "We're looking for Darryl."

While he was talking, the shorter guy went over to Darryl's suitcases.

"One of the professors is missing some important papers," the tall one continued. "They're in an extra-large black briefcase. Have you seen anything like that around here?"

Chapter 2

So Darryl was a thief! I have to admit I was surprised. Sure, the guy was a little weird—but a *thief*? I was about to answer when I glanced over at the shorter man. Somehow, he'd already made a long slit in Darryl's suitcase. Now he was pulling something out of it, a satisfied grin on his face. I could hardly believe my eyes. It was the strange contraption Darryl was using when I thought I'd been dreaming!

But what was *with* these guys? They had no right to trash Darryl's stuff. Something fishy was going on here. "Hey! You guys aren't security!" I yelled. "Get out of here before I call the police!" I went for the phone.

The tall guy stepped behind me and

threw his arm across my chest. His grip was like iron. Then something hard pressed against my neck, and sharp pains shot through me like knives. I wanted to scream—but I couldn't even open my mouth. I couldn't move. My legs turned to jelly, but his iron-like arm held me up.

"Tell me everything you know about Darryl *and* the briefcase," he barked. "Then I'll let you go."

I saw everything through a fog of pain. Then, suddenly, Darryl was there— charging across the room. The smaller guy dropped Darryl's contraption. It fell to the floor and smashed with the tinkling sound of breaking glass.

Darryl whipped out a short tube and held it in front of the desk lamp. In a split second, a beam of light shot out of the tube toward the short guy's stomach. Somehow, the hot ray of light covered the guy like a cocoon! Then the floor seemed to rise up in front of me, and suddenly everything went black.

When I opened my eyes, I had a terrible headache. Spots danced before my eyes, as if they'd been dazzled by a dozen flash bulbs.

Darryl helped me up off the floor. "Nick! Are you going to be all right?" he asked. His face looked concerned and sincerely sympathetic.

"I'm about half blind—but otherwise I'm okay," I said. The pain had gone. The spots were slowly fading away.

"What's that smell?" I said. The strange odor in the room was awful.

Darryl pointed. On the floor were scraps of blackened clothes and tiny bits of shoes and a belt.

"Is the guy—" I said.

"He is destroyed," Darryl said flatly. "But the other one escaped." His small mouth was taut with worry.

I couldn't believe it. Had he actually *zapped* that guy?

"Why are they after you?" I asked.

Darryl sat on the bed, the briefcase on his knees. "I had hoped to keep you out of this. But that will no longer be possible. Nick, I'm not—uh—*from* here. The guys you saw, they're my enemies," he said. "They blew apart my planet in the last great space war. Our cities, our families, *everything*—were ripped to pieces and scattered in space! Only a few of us escaped before the final moment. And I have a treasure to guard. *Look!*"

He opened the briefcase. I looked inside and felt I might fall forward into the deep cloud of swirling colors. Through greens and blues and yellows I could see tiny eyes. There seemed to be *thousands* of them. Dizzily, I looked up at Darryl as he shut the briefcase.

"They are ready to grow," he said. "When they do, there will be enough for us to start again—in a new place."

I was beginning to get the picture. "You risked your own people's future to save me," I said in wonderment.

"Those two would have killed you— for no good reason," he said.

"But now they know where you are," I said. "You're still in danger."

He nodded his head. "I must leave. I need a safe place to hide until my friends come for me," he said.

"I'll help you!" I cried. "I grew up right here in San Francisco. There's no place around this town that I don't know about," I said.

He looked at me for a long moment. His fingers moved nervously over the handle of the briefcase.

"Tonight I must be at Point Reyes. Can you hide me until then?" he asked.

"Yes, but we'll need a car," I said. I thought hard. My mom worked across the bay. It would take her an hour to get here. Then I thought of Mike. "I met a really nice guy yesterday. He has a car. I'm sure he'd let me borrow it," I said. "Stay here, Darryl. Chill out. I'll be back as soon as I can."

As Darryl watched me leave, I saw that the expression on his face was trusting and hopeful. I felt a great weight settle on my shoulders. If we failed . . .

I rushed down the stairs toward Mike's room, but then I stopped. Kara! She was smart and resourceful. I wanted her with me.

Luckily, she was alone. She grinned when she saw me at her door. "Couldn't stand to be away from me for a whole hour, huh?" she teased.

I sat beside her on the floor where she was sorting a pile of books. "Kara, listen to me. Something, uh—*amazing* has happened, and I want you to help me," I said. What else could I do? I told her everything—about the strange visitors, the fight, and Darryl's briefcase. I watched her face as I spoke. She looked shocked when I told her about Darryl killing one of his enemies. But she didn't say anything. She just kept staring at me with an alert, serious expression on her face.

"You believe me, don't you?" I said when I'd finished.

"Yes," she said.

"I knew it! I *knew* I could count on you!" I grabbed her by the shoulders and quickly kissed her on the mouth.

"I'm going to see if I can borrow a car now," I explained. "Meet me in my room in about 15 minutes. And bring some food and warm clothes, okay? We're going to hide out for a few hours before we head for Point Reyes."

She nodded, and I left.

No one was in Mike's room, so I ran right back to my own room. Darryl was clearly alarmed.

"*You told her!*" he gasped.

"It's okay!" I said. "I'm smart about people. Believe me, we can trust her!"

At that moment I heard a knock. I opened the door for Kara. She glanced at Darryl nervously. Then she took my hand and drew me out into the hallway.

"Nick, I like you," she said. "You're a really nice person. Now, I want you to understand that what I've done is for your own good. You need help, *serious* help—right now.

"I've called the police, Nick. They're coming to take you to the hospital. And they're going to put Darryl where he won't pose a danger to other people."

Chapter 3

I hid my face in my hands so she wouldn't see my shock and anger. Then after a moment I said, "You're right." I know my voice sounded upset, but that was okay. I took deep, loud breaths. It gave me time to think.

Then, before Kara knew what was happening, I quickly backed into my room and locked the door.

Kara started pounding on the door. "Nick! Let me in!" she yelled. "Do you hear me? Let me *in!*"

I ran to the window and pulled it open. "Darryl! Grab your briefcase!" I whispered. Then I yanked off my belt and looped it over the clothesline, gripping the ends in my hands. I climbed up on the windowsill.

"Wait until I jump off," I said to Darryl. "This line isn't strong enough to hold both of us."

Darryl looked bewildered, but he nodded and said nothing.

I pushed myself over the windowsill. Across the way, Kara's window was just a little lower than mine. That downward angle was all it took to send me zooming between the two buildings, the air whistling against my ears. When Kara's window was just inches away, I twisted my body away from the wall. Then, a moment after my feet touched the windowpane, I felt my body rocketing through the window in a shower of broken glass. I landed on my hands and knees, bleeding from a dozen tiny cuts.

I scrambled to my feet and looked out. Darryl was leaning over the sill in our room, ready to go. "Don't look down!" I called. He pushed himself over the windowsill, one arm grabbing his belt, the other clutching his briefcase. For a moment he hesitated, staring down at the long drop to the concrete below. Then he took off, zooming straight for the wall. At the last second, he twisted toward the window—but not soon enough. His shoulder rammed into the wall. On impact, Darryl let out a strange kind of whistle, which I thought must be a sound of pain. I had to reach out and grab his other arm to yank him inside.

He was breathing hard. "That was fearsome!" he said, rubbing his shoulder.

"Told you not to look," I said.

Then I quickly rummaged through Kara's drawers and found a sweatshirt to hide the cuts on my arms.

"Where can we hide?" Darryl cried.

"I'm thinking of a place downtown," I said as I pulled the sweatshirt over my head. "Let's get going."

"Will we take the bus?" he said.

"Yes—but we won't get on at the stop right outside," I said. "They'll be looking for us. Come on, let's go!"

We took the back way out of the building. From there we had to run around some parking lots and tennis courts and a big playing field.

Finally, we climbed over a hurricane fence and hurried past a row of squat maintenance buildings. Luckily, we were surrounded by big eucalyptus trees. I noticed that signs on the buildings said, *DANGER, NO ADMITTANCE*. The place seemed deserted. Then I heard a low, menacing growl behind us.

The dog wasn't huge, but he looked heavy and strong. He seemed to have no neck at all, just thick cords of muscle. The animal walked slowly toward us, making a deep rumbling growl.

"Why is it threatening us?" Darryl asked quietly.

"He's been trained to guard this area," I explained.

"Okay," said Darryl, his hand slowly reaching into his pocket.

"*Okay?*" I cried. I picked up a stick that was lying on the ground and started to wave it at the angry-looking dog.

With a snarl, the dog leaped at me, grabbing the stick in his mouth. From the corner of my eye, I could see that Darryl was holding the tube he'd used last night. But then the dog let go of the stick and leaped at my stomach, knocking me to the ground. The next thing I knew his paws were on my chest, pushing me down like heavy lead weights. I could feel his hot breath in my face.

Suddenly a beam of bright, hot light shot out, just missing the dog's ear. The surprised animal yelped and bounded away from me. For a moment he just stood back, looking confused. Then, with a loud whine, he ran off behind a building, his tail between his legs.

Still shaking with fear, I got to my feet. "Way to go, Darryl! How'd you do that?" I asked him.

He showed me the tube and a penlight he'd taken from my room. "When you capture light from another source, the tube channels the rays into power," he said.

"Do your enemies have tubes like that?" I asked.

"No," he said grimly. "Their weapons are *worse*," he said.

Darryl was huffing and puffing by the time we reached a thickly wooded area. It was slow going. But we went on, climbing over fallen eucalyptus branches and tangled vines.

Finally we reached the street that bordered the shopping district. "Okay, we'll hide in there for a while," I said, pointing to the mall.

"But that place will be bursting with people!" said Darryl.

"That's the point!" I said. "It's hard to spot someone in a crowd. We'll hide your briefcase in a shopping bag."

Darryl looked worried. "Nick," he

said, "your judgment has not been—uh—perfect so far," he said.

"Oh, yeah?" I demanded. "Wasn't that clothesline a great way to escape?"

"But what about your friend, Kara?" he asked, shaking his head. "You are wrong about people."

"I'm *not*! Just her. But even if I was wrong about her, I'm right about this. Or do you have a better idea?" I snapped.

"We can hide among the trees until night," he suggested.

"*You* can sit in the cold, drippy trees for hours," I said. "I'm starving."

"You are not a waiting person," he said. "But you have clever ways to break free. I'll come with you."

I felt guilty. Hiding in the trees was probably an okay plan. I should have let Darryl call the shots. After all, he was the one with so much at stake. But the thought of staring at tree trunks for hours made me feel a little crazy.

The mall was pretty full—the way it

almost always is in the early evening. Everybody was out of school and off work. The food court was jammed. I had to wait for quite a while to get a burrito.

"Don't you ever eat?" I asked Darryl.

Darryl's beady little eyes sparkled. "Oh, yes, Nick. I'm eating now," he said with a little smile.

"*Huh?*" I said, staring at him. Darryl was just standing there, talking. Nothing was going into his mouth but air!

"Our bodies absorb food in a different way. It goes through a special belt we wear under our clothes," Darryl said. "Would you like to see it?"

Usually I'm pretty curious, but I said no. All I could think about was my own empty stomach. I was half finished with my burrito when a cop walked by. He didn't seem to pay attention to us, but just the sight of him made me nervous.

"Let's go," I said.

"I thought you said we were hidden in the crowd, Nick. Why are you so

29

restless?" Darryl asked, looking worried.

"That guy in blue," I said. "He's a cop, a policeman."

We went down the escalator to the rotunda. On the way down I saw *another* cop walking beside the second-floor railing. Or was it the same cop?

We reached the rotunda. Dozens of grownups and kids were sitting around the fountain—including another cop.

"Wait a minute," I said to Darryl. I looked around and counted three more cops on the ground floor. Two more were leaning over the second-floor railing—looking directly at us.

Chapter 4

Darryl was no fool. He figured out what was happening right away. "They want to capture us," he said. Before I could say a word, he pulled the penlight and tube from his pocket.

His hand moved so fast I couldn't tell where he was aiming. Then beams of light shot out in three directions. The water in the big fountain was suddenly boiling, sending up a blinding cloud of steam! Screaming in alarm, people jumped off the benches, pulling their kids away from the hot water.

At the same time, the front window of a video store buckled from the heat and collapsed in jagged shards. Shoppers shrieked and were backing away from the broken glass just as a potted tree behind us caught fire. And all of this happened in about three seconds!

The entire mall erupted in chaos. All around us, parents were yelling and frantically trying to herd their kids to safety. Other shoppers were screaming and running—even knocking people down in their mad rush toward the exits. A few people called for calm, trying to keep the panic down.

I saw one cop stand up on the bench surrounding the fountain. His cold eyes were directly focused on Darryl! But then we were swept away in a wave of people. The next time I looked, a cop was waving everyone toward the rear exit. "No running!" his voice boomed. "Everybody move along nice and orderly, and no one's gonna get hurt."

We blended into the excited crowd and followed them through the door. A lot of people in the crowd headed for the bus stop.

"The cops will be watching the

buses," I said. "Let's walk down the street a ways before we get on." How cool was *that*? I'd show Darryl that I could be patient.

For 10 minutes or so we walked through the neighborhood streets. We heard sirens coming from the direction of the mall, but the streets themselves were quiet.

"What is this place you want to go to next?" said Darryl.

"It's called a printing plant. It's where they print newspapers and load them on trucks to be delivered. My dad used to work there."

"And he works there no longer?" Darryl asked curiously.

"Nah. He got fired after he and my mom broke up," I said.

Darryl looked confused. "Could you explain *fired* and *broke up*?" he asked.

"Sure thing. *Fired* means he was doing a bad job so they made him leave. *Broke up* means that he and Mom don't live together anymore," I said.

"I'm sorry. That is a sad thing for all of you," Darryl said kindly.

"He ran out on us," I said. "I don't care if I ever see him again."

After an hour, I figured it was safe for us to get on a bus. By now it was almost dark, and the bus was half-empty. There weren't many passengers. Just a few teenagers heading home from the mall, and some tired-looking parents juggling kids and shopping bags. I couldn't believe it. Only a few hours earlier I was just a guy with homework to do and a date with Kara to look forward to. Now, that seemed like at least a year ago!

There was a faint buzzing in the air. A tiny insect passed behind Darryl's neck. Darryl turned and made a low whistling noise, his eyes wide.

"*It's a spy device!*" he whispered. "Can you hit it with water?"

"Water? I don't have any," I said.

Darryl quickly reached over to a girl

in jogging clothes, sitting across the aisle. He grabbed her water bottle. "Excuse me," he said. "My friend will pay you for your water."

"Hey!" the girl cried out. "What's the idea? Give that back!"

Frantically, Darryl started squirting streams of water at the bug. "I keep missing it! Help me, Nick!" he cried. The passengers sitting around us backed away from him. "What do you think you're doing?" a big kid demanded.

Just ahead of me a baby girl in her mother's arms was sucking on a bottle. I grabbed it out of her hands. "Sorry, I really need this!" I sputtered. The baby threw back her head and shrieked.

I squeezed the bottle hard—squirting milk everywhere but on the bug!

The baby's mother kicked out at me. "You jerk!" she cried. Then she handed the little girl to her older sister and stood up. I gulped. She was a lot bigger than me.

"You're getting me wet!" an old man

sitting across the aisle snarled at me.

"What's going on back there?" the bus driver shouted.

"It's a malaria mosquito!" I yelled. "We've got to kill it!"

The baby's mother slapped her hands together next to Darryl's ear. Then she cried out, "Auugh!"—as if she were more surprised than hurt. She opened her hands, swearing. The tiny gray thing was stuck to the palm of her hand, which was rapidly turning red. Darryl doused the bug with water. Then he picked it up carefully and dropped it into his shirt pocket. The mom scowled at Darryl. "*Idiot!*" she snorted.

And then the bus slowly groaned to a stop, and the driver walked back toward us. "All right," she said in a bored, put-upon voice. "What's all the commotion about?"

Darryl and I ran toward the exit, but the big kid stepped out and blocked our way. "Oh, no you don't!" he said.

I didn't know what to do! So I squirted his face with a stream of milk from the baby's bottle. "You little creep!" he yelled, grabbing for me. Then Darryl put his hand on the guy's shoulder. The boy gasped and backed up. I knew what Darryl had done to him. And I knew from personal experience just how that shock felt.

Barreling out the open door, we ran across the street. We kept on running the neighborhood streets until we were panting for breath.

"I thought humans were about 65 percent water," Darryl said. "Why didn't you use your *own* water?"

"Oh. Um, we just can't aim it that well. Watch." I held my finger a couple of feet from my mouth, spit, and missed.

A look of pity came over Darryl's face. "Oh, dear. That's a skill you need to improve," he said, trying to be polite.

"It's no biggie, Darryl. Don't worry. We, uh, humans don't usually defend ourselves with water," I assured him. "Now let's see that spy thing."

He reached into his shirt pocket and held his hand out. I peered at the tiny thing in his palm. It was *really* tiny— about the size of a grain of rice. I squinted and held the "flying bug" closer to see it better. It was a gray cylinder with one glassy eye.

"That's the recording part of the device," Darryl said in a worried voice. "They know where we are."

Chapter 5

"If they know where we are, we'd better get moving," I said. Luckily, we were close to downtown. I was able to wave down a taxi in a few minutes.

"You know where the newspaper printing plant is?" I asked the driver.

"Never heard of it," he said.

I gave the cabbie directions. Very few people seem to know about the place—which was why I thought we might be safe there.

It only took about 15 minutes to get to the printing plant. To get to the main building, we walked past the long parking lot full of delivery trucks.

At the guard station, we had to check in at the front desk.

"Hello, ma'am. I'm here to see Chuck

Gunnison," I said, smiling politely.

"Your name, please?" asked the security guard. A nametag on her crisp blue uniform read "Bonita."

I told her my real name because I couldn't think fast enough to come up with another one. "Yes, ma'am, I'm Nick de la Fuente," I said.

"Oh! Go right on in," she said with a smile. "Chuck should be in the mailroom."

"Chuck knows all the drivers real well," I told Darryl. "He'll get us a ride out to Point Reyes."

"What's in there?" Darryl asked. We were walking down a hallway next to a glass wall. On the other side of the glass we could see the giant machines in the pressroom.

"Look, Darryl, it's really interesting. This is where all the pages of the newspaper get printed," I said.

Inside the room were 22 machines called press units. Each held huge rolls of paper that spun through on metal rollers. The units were as tall as houses. Guys who worked up on a press unit had to climb a ladder to get to the top. When I was a little kid, I had really been impressed that my dad worked here, among these huge machines. I was sure he must be very important.

Next we walked into the mailroom. I explained how it all worked to Darryl: "Look—when the newspapers leave the pressroom, they come out here, one by one, on a conveyor belt. Then some different machines stack and tie the papers into bundles. After that, the conveyor loads them directly into the backs of the waiting trucks."

I walked up to the foreman. "Is Chuck around?" I asked.

"He just went to the pressroom to get a batch of earplugs," said the foreman. "He should be back in a minute or so."

I didn't want to wait, so back we went to the pressroom.

A red and white machine that looked like an oversize bumper car quietly glided up behind Darryl.

"Heads up, Darryl!" I said. "That's an AGV, an Automatic Guided Vehicle. Isn't it *neat*? It's controlled by electric wires embedded in the floor."

AGVs are used to carry the huge rolls of paper to the press units. Each roll weighs about 1,800 pounds. If you stretched out all the paper on a roll, it would be seven miles long!

I glanced around, looking for Chuck. Instead I saw a man with a clipboard. He seemed to be directing people to different tasks. Oh, no! It was *Dad*.

"Nick!" He walked up to us quickly, then stopped. "I thought that was you," he said. We stared at each other.

"All grown up," he said quietly.

"This is your father?" Darryl said, looking panicked.

"Yeah—grown up without you," I said to Dad.

"Yeah."

"We can't stay here, Nick," Darryl whispered. "They'll find us here for sure! Believe me, my friend—they search every connection!" he said.

"Okay, we'll get going!" I said.

For once, my dad actually seemed to be worried about me. "What's going on, Nick? Are you in some kind of trouble?" he asked. Then he looked at Darryl suspiciously, as if he was waiting for an explanation.

Darryl ignored him. "Hold your hand forward," he cried.

I did. Being careful not to touch me, Darryl dropped something in my hand. It was a metallic-looking container about the size of a matchbox.

"If the briefcase is destroyed," he explained, "take this container to the lighthouse at Point Reyes tonight. My friends will take it from you."

"Say, what is that—*drugs*?" said Dad. Now he looked really angry.

"No way!" I snapped. "Look, Dad, we're leaving now. I came here to see Chuck, anyway."

"Give me the box, Nick," Dad said sternly. "I'm still your father!"

But just then a skinny guy with a gray beard came running up to Dad. His eyes were wide, his mouth hanging open.

"There you are, Mr. de la Fuente," he gasped. "Thank God! These strange guys came to the guard station a few minutes ago. Bonita tried to stop them—" He shook his head and tried to catch his breath. "I think she's dead."

"What are you saying?" Dad cried. "Where are the men now?"

Both of us caught sight of them at the same time. Darryl let out a loud whistle. They were here—standing just inside the pressroom door!

There were four of them; they all looked like brothers. One held a long, pole-like object the size of a baseball bat.

44

Another security guard was running toward them, his gun in the air. "Hold it!" he shouted. "Hold it right there!"

The alien with the pole pointed it toward the guard. Instantly, a blast of blinding white light shot out, and the guard was gone—along with a blackened chunk of the concrete floor.

All over the pressroom, people were running and yelling and ducking behind the press units. One guy hit a lever on an AGV. That released a huge roll of paper from its pins. Now it fell with a deafening boom that shook the floor. As if it had been aimed, it rolled straight toward the aliens, whacking one on the shoulder. He staggered, but he didn't seem interested in what had hit him. The aliens were looking around for Darryl.

From the corner of my eye, I saw Darryl run up a ladder. He grabbed the tube from his pocket and held it up. But *they* had seen him, too.

The alien holding the pole aimed at

the closest press unit. One of the metal rollers collapsed and melted instantly. With a sickening groan, the unit came to a grinding stop.

Then, down the line, like dominos, the rolling wheels of *all* the units halted with terrible jolting, scraping sounds. Half-printed newspaper pages came loose and floated to the floor.

One end of Darryl's ladder came loose and swung in a narrow arc. A woman screamed as the falling ladder flew past her face, missing her by inches. Darryl held on with one arm, the briefcase clutched to his chest.

An alien grabbed hold of one of the pressmen. Then the alien with the pole held the weapon to the back of the man's head. As Darryl slowly lowered the tube, the other two aliens pulled him roughly away from the ladder. They yanked the briefcase from his hand and hustled him out toward the loading dock. He turned and gave me a desperate look I'll never forget. The look said, "*Please. . . .*"

As they reached the front door, the alien with the weapon turned and looked quickly around the room. Then he stared up at the ceiling, as if he were studying it. He slowly raised the tip of the pole.

"*Run!*" I screamed.

Streaks of light shot toward the support beams. Then, from out of nowhere, Dad appeared and grabbed my arm. "This way!" he yelled. We ran out toward the loading dock.

Screams and shouts rang out behind us. A man yelling, "Larry! Larry!" brushed past me. As he looked around desperately, his frightened face almost collided with mine.

Then I could hear terrible cracking and tearing sounds as the roof beams began to collapse. Finally, there was a deep rumble as the ceiling started to shift and break apart.

As we reached the loading dock, I

saw Darryl's tube lying on the ground. My heart sank. I pulled away from Dad and grabbed it.

Right next to me, a chunk of wood and plaster the size of a bathtub hit the floor and broke apart in a cloud of dust. Dodging it just in time, I ran under the huge metal door of the loading dock.

It was a seven-foot jump from the dock to the pavement. I ran to the nearest truck, yanking open the driver's side door.

I'd just gotten the truck started when Dad climbed in the other side.

"What are you doing?" he cried.

"Leave me alone!" I snapped angrily. I tried to shove him away, but he grabbed my arms and held them fast. I had forgotten how strong he was. He glared at me.

"You're *not* going to Point Reyes!" Dad said.

Chapter 6

I pulled loose from Dad's grip and glared at him. "I *am* going," I said quietly. He looked like he wanted to say something, but he kept quiet.

I tried to back the truck out of the parking lot. But people were swarming out of the loading dock all around me. Then, suddenly, with a great rolling boom, the entire roof of the printing plant folded inward and caved in on itself! A huge cloud of dirty brown dust rose in the sky.

Turning the truck around slowly, I headed for the street. Three men and a woman hurried beside the truck, carrying a man with a bloody chest.

At the street, I stopped. "Okay, Dad, you can get out here," I said.

"No," he said.

"You should stay here to help out," I said. "There are injured people inside!"

"I'm staying with you," he said.

"Huh. That will be a change from the last three years," I snapped.

We drove across town in silence. The streetlights were just coming on. Wealthy people drove by in their shiny, quiet cars. No doubt they were headed for restaurants and theaters. Homeless people were setting up blankets and sleeping bags in doorways.

Finally, we left the city and crossed the Golden Gate Bridge. Dense fog was turning the strings of lights between the towers a fuzzy orange color. The Point Reyes lighthouse would be working tonight, for sure.

I glanced over at Dad. The dark outline of his face looked so familiar, yet so remote. I realized that I didn't know him anymore. Finally we got off the bridge and onto the freeway.

"Dad, I really don't want you to come. You'll just be interfering."

"They could kill you!" said Dad. "Whatever this is, it's too much for a kid like you to get mixed up in."

"But Darryl saved my life!" I cried.

"Who *is* Darryl?" he asked.

I didn't answer. I just looked out over the lights of Mill Valley. I knew the turnoff for Point Reyes would be coming up soon.

Dad put his hand on my arm. "Give me a chance, won't you? Tell me what's going on, Nick. I promise I'll listen."

So I did. I told him everything. And as I talked, the smell of the dead alien's charred clothes sprang fresh in my mind. I showed him Darryl's tube. "I have to get it back to him," I said. "Maybe he still has a chance to beat these guys somehow."

Dad said, "I want to help you."

"That's a new one," I said.

There was a long silence. Then he

said, "Believe me, Nick. I *wanted* to help you—and your mom."

"Then why *didn't* you?" I burst out. Suddenly, I didn't feel so angry. I felt like crying.

"Listen to me, now," Dad said. "This is important. When my drinking got out of hand, everything slid away—my job, the house, and you and Mom.

"Finally, my boss said he'd give me one more chance if I joined a support group and quit drinking. I've done that, son. And I've started climbing out of my hole. It's taken me a year."

"Are you cured?" I said.

"Not *cured*, no. I still want a drink nearly every day—sometimes every hour," he said with a shy smile. "But I haven't had a drink in two years." He sighed. "I want you to know that I *thought* about you and Mom all the time. But I was too ashamed to show my face—after what I'd done."

I thought of all the times I'd wished

he was dead. There were so many nights that he'd come home drunk and stupid. Pretty soon I started blaming him for *everything* bad that happened: for not being able to afford a dog; for not helping me with my homework; for every time Mom cried.

We were out in the country now. I could see the dim outline of the hills against the night sky. Houses were few, and traffic had thinned out. Then I noticed a car quickly closing in behind us—a police car. My hands tightened on the wheel.

Dad saw it, too. "Get in the back," he said, "under the papers."

He reached out and took the wheel as I slid over the back of the driver's seat. I was pulling bundles of papers over my body just as the cops turned on their lights and signaled Dad to pull over to the side of the road.

There I lay as still as I could, watching the rotating light on the cops' car wash over the ceiling of the truck. I could hear the crunch of gravel as an officer walked up to the truck.

"Good evening. I need to see some identification," said the officer.

"Sure," said Dad. "Anything wrong with the truck?"

The officer didn't answer. He frowned as he studied Dad's ID.

"This ID says that you're a foreman. How come you're driving a truck?" the officer asked.

I did a double take. *What?* My dad, the loser, was a *foreman*?

Dad said, "The guy who usually has this run came down with the flu. I owe him, so I'm helping him out tonight."

"What time did you leave the plant?" said the officer.

There was a small, awkward pause. I could almost hear the wheels turning in Dad's head. Then he spoke calmly.

"I didn't look at the clock, but this run leaves about 8:10." Dad said.

"You must have missed all the excitement," said the officer. "Did you know that the whole printing plant was destroyed tonight?"

"*What?*" Dad cried out. He sounded pretty convincing to me.

"Yeah, it's *gone*. No one knows for sure what happened. But something knocked out all the support beams, and the roof caved in. Three people dead that we know of. About a dozen injured. They're still searching the wreckage," said the officer. "I hear they're looking at possible sabotage."

"I can't believe it," said Dad slowly.

"Don't suppose you met anybody named Darryl hanging around the plant today?" asked the officer.

"Hmmm. There was a Darryl working part time a few months back, but he quit," Dad answered.

Then a couple of cars went by, and whatever the officer said, I missed. But suddenly the bright beam of a flashlight was sweeping through the back of the truck. I froze. If the officer climbed in and did a thorough search, he'd find me for sure. But after a few moments, the flashlight clicked off. I took a deep breath and relaxed.

Dad and the cop exchanged a few more words. At last, I heard the truck's engine rev up and Dad drove away.

I pushed my way out from under the newspapers. "Stay back there," Dad said without turning his head. "I think they're following us."

Chapter 7

We drove on, both of us thinking hard. "What are we going to do?" I finally said.

"Let's see if they stick with us as far as Point Reyes. We'll keep moving until we get a mile or so from the lighthouse. Then I'll park the truck and we'll walk. I'll pick a spot where hiking trails fan out in several directions."

I remembered now that we used to come to Point Reyes a lot—all three of us, as a family. Dad and I would race along the beach. He'd always let me win, and then pretend he was going to throw me in the water. Mom took dozens of pictures. Unless she threw them away, they're still in an album somewhere.

After about half an hour, Dad said, "Okay, we're on Point Reyes."

"Are the cops still there?" I asked.

"I'm not sure," he said.

I wondered how much information the cops actually had. Had they connected Darryl with the death at San Francisco State? How much had Kara told them? Did they know anything about me?

The truck slowed down and stopped. We were in a small parking lot that I recognized. From that lot, I remembered, several trails led off toward the beach and the hills.

Then I saw a black-and-white police car slowly coming up the road.

"Let's go," I said.

"Wait," Dad said. "There's a tool kit up here in the glove compartment. I want to find some kind of weapon." He rummaged around and pulled out a wrench, which he stuck in his jacket.

"Aw, come on. What good is that

thing gonna do?" I said with a frown.

"I don't know. Maybe I could throw it if I had to," said Dad.

We jumped out of the truck just as the police car turned off the road. We ducked behind some bushes and watched. The black-and-white slowly turned around in the parking lot and drove back out to the road.

If they were really looking for us, why hadn't they parked and followed one of the trails? Or had they seen us and gone for help? Worry settled in my stomach like a cold, heavy ball.

We hurried along in the dark, stumbling over low bushes and clumps of grass. Down a steep cliff in front of us was a narrow beach. Through the fog, I could see the ghostly white of breaking waves.

A few cars went by. Each time one approached, we flattened ourselves on the ground until the taillights grew dim in the distance.

Finally, we rounded a bend. "There it is," Dad said in a low voice. About a mile away, we could see the lights of the lighthouse turning slowly, their wide rays shimmering softly over the waves.

I put my hand on Dad's arm. "Stop!" I muttered. I thought I heard footsteps.

Suddenly, a small herd of deer bounded across the pavement and down the hill toward the beach. Then powerful beams of light blinded us from two directions.

"Walk up to the road slowly, your hands in front of you," a voice called out. Then I saw the guy. He was the cop who had pulled Dad over.

There were two of them. One man was pretty chunky, with gray hair at the temples. The other looked even younger than me. They pushed Dad aside and focused on me. First, they read me my rights. Then I think they said they were taking me in for questioning—regarding possible sabotage and a murder at San

Francisco State! I hardly heard them. I felt like I was caught in a bad dream.

The young guy frisked me from head to toe. The older one stepped away and opened the back door of the police car.

"I'm coming, too," said Dad. "That boy's a minor—and I'm his father." It gave me a chill. I never thought I'd be glad to hear him say that.

They put Dad and me in the back seat of the police car. I looked at the metal screen that separated the cops from the back seat and thought of cages. For a moment, I felt pure panic. What would they do to me? How could I ever help Darryl now? I thought of the tube in my pocket. I wished I'd had the presence of mind to throw it away.

The older cop drove. As the car turned around and started pulling away from the lighthouse, another car passed us. Peering into the dark interior, I saw Darryl's pale face! "There he is!" I cried out. "Darryl's in that car!"

The cops turned around and flashed their lights, but the car sped on. The cop used his microphone. "Pull over to the side of the road," he boomed.

This time the car pulled over, and the police car pulled up behind it. The older cop turned to his partner. He gave him a look that seemed to say, "Take it easy." Then he drew his pistol, holding it discreetly by his side as he stepped out of the car.

The young cop turned and motioned for us to stay where we were. "You two just sit tight and keep quiet," he said.

We watched as the older cop leaned over the car. I couldn't make out the words he was saying, but he sounded firm and fair. Everyone in the car stepped out, including Darryl. They all seemed calm. I didn't see the pole weapon anywhere.

The older cop said something to Darryl, who stepped forward. Then the cop put his hand on Darryl's arm.

"Ow!" he yelled.

The younger cop leaped out of the police car, his gun drawn. "All of you! Hands in the air!" he shouted.

But one of the aliens quickly reached back into the car. I saw the pole weapon shining brightly in the headlights.

"Watch out!" I yelled. Dad and I dropped to the floor of the police car.

A blinding light flooded over us just before the aliens' car sped away.

Dad and I scrambled out of the police car. There was a big blackened hole where the cops had been standing! The smell of burned clothing filled the air. The two police officers had been *destroyed*, as Darryl would have said. Had Darryl been destroyed, too?

Chapter 8

I stood in the middle of the road, feeling exhausted and helpless.

Dad said, "Let's wait until they're out of sight. Then we'll follow them."

"How? Do you mean we'll just *walk* the rest of the way?" I said.

"Nah," said Dad. "Let's take this." He jerked his head at the police car.

"You're kidding!" I said. "That's gotta be totally illegal."

Dad almost laughed. "Nick," he said, "we can hardly be more illegal than we are already."

We. Dad wasn't in this mess nearly as deep as I was. Yet he had said *we.*

When the aliens' car was out of sight, we took off after them. I didn't feel much better sitting on the front side of the divider screen in the police car. The dispatcher's voice kept coming on the radio, telling us to check in. I knew it wouldn't be long before more cop cars showed up.

We drove up the steep hill until the road ended. The rest of the way to the beach—up over the top of the hill and down to the light—we traveled on foot.

We walked quickly past the visitors' center. Then we climbed over the tall cyclone fence they always closed at midnight. We didn't worry much about being quiet. The wind and the waves crashing on the rocks would drown out all but the loudest noise.

For a moment we hid behind a rock and peered around. Just below us were the steps leading down to the lights. There are 310 of those steps. I know, because when I was a kid, I counted them every time I came. Added up, those steps are the equivalent of a 30-story building.

At the bottom of the steps was the historic old lighthouse. And right on top of a small building was the modern light—the one they use now. The old light had a lens with a thousand prisms. The new one, however, is small and simple—just two thousand-watt bulbs encased in two revolving lights.

As we looked down the hill, I thought I saw something moving near the building with the lights.

I heard Darryl's strange whistle. "That's *him!*" I said to Dad. "Darryl is either hurt or afraid."

"Let's get off the walkway and go along the cliff," said Dad.

We climbed down by crawling over the rocks. The light helped us see what was just ahead of us, but it was tough going. Several times I slipped on the jagged rocks. Each time I slid a few feet before I reached something to grab onto. I didn't look down.

When we were down as far as the

lights, Dad grabbed my arm. "Let's get over there. Then maybe we can see what's going on," he whispered.

Slowly, we inched ourselves up the cliff to the walkway and positioned ourselves behind the building. Just above us, about 12 feet away, the lights revolved slowly. I peered around the building and saw the aliens.

They were tying Darryl to the handrail with what looked like thin string. I gasped. One of Darryl's sleeves hung limp and empty. He was missing an arm! His other arm still clutched the big black briefcase.

Once he was tied, the aliens retreated down the opposite side of the cliff. As they went over, they searched the sky.

Dad and I looked, too. *"There!"* I whispered.

Through the dense fog, we could make out a small revolving light, glowing faintly. As the light turned, its rays seemed to flicker from different surfaces, like a sparkling jewel.

An alien head peeked over the cliff. He was aiming the pole toward the sky. I wanted to scream. How could I destroy the pole? I had *nothing*—not even a penlight to shine through the tube!

Light shot out from the pole, piercing the fog. The jeweled light shot back into the darkness. Darryl closed his eyes.

Suddenly it came to me. "Dad!" I whispered. "Boost me up on the roof!"

For once, he didn't question me. He immediately gave me a leg up.

I climbed up as quietly as I could. "Hand me the wrench!" I hissed.

Dad shoved the wrench in my hand. With all my strength, I started yanking on the bolts that secured the lights. They wouldn't budge.

Dad saw my problem. "Nick! Help me up!" he said in a low voice.

I held onto the base of a light, leaned down, and stuck out my hand. In a second Dad had hauled himself up and began to work on loosening the bolts.

But just then, the whole roof lit up. A booming voice from the top of the steps called out: "*Police!* We see you. Come down from the building at once."

I looked up. At the top of the steps were the silhouettes of half a dozen armed cops.

But before we had a chance to respond, I noticed a movement from the cliff. I turned. The jewel-like light had come in closer and closer. Now it seemed almost near enough to touch. Then a tremendous bolt of light shot out from the cliff. The flickering jewel shattered into a shower of fragments!

An alien raised up from the cliff and aimed the pole again. This time he was pointing toward Darryl.

"No!" I yelled. "*No!*"

But another bolt of light shot from the pole, and the briefcase melted and turned black. For an instant, I saw a mist of colors, and a thousand eyes. Then the sad-looking eyes closed and there was nothing—nothing at all—in the cold night air.

Chapter 9

Darryl's head dropped forward. I was sure he'd been killed.

Behind me, Dad said, "It's loose!"

I turned and stared in disbelief. He had loosened the bracket holding one of the lights!

I jerked the light around to focus the beam on the cliff. The intense beam highlighted every rock and pebble. It turned the aliens' faces paper white.

I could see them staring at me. One of them raised the pole.

I yanked the tube from my pocket and held it in front of the light. A thousand watts of power poured through the tube and hit the cliff like a rocket. Each one of the aliens was caught in his own cocoon of fiery light. Then the brilliant cocoons winked out. In a moment, ragged pieces of scorched clothing drifted off the cliff and into the sea.

I dropped down off the roof and ran to Darryl. Dad was behind me, a few paces back. We yanked at the strings that held him, but they were like iron. Slowly, Darryl lifted his head.

"Darryl!" I cried.

Darryl opened his eyes. The howling wind slapped his empty sleeve against my hand.

"Your arm—what happened to your arm?" I cried out.

"My arm and I broke up," he said, trying to smile. "Ah, my friend, Nick. Here you are at last! Do you have the small box I gave you?"

"Yes!" I said. I took it out of my pocket and showed it to him.

"Put it in my hand, please," he said. I closed his fingers over it and felt a mild shock.

His eyes glowed. "I was right about

you. I knew you were the one," he said.

He looked up at the sky. I did, too, but I saw nothing. What was he seeing?

"There's another," Dad said quietly.

Peeping through the fog was another jeweled light, coming closer, closer. I wanted to touch it. It grew very bright. Then waves of colors—aqua, gold, violet, crimson, and blue—washed over us. The box in Darryl's hand opened. Two pairs of eyes rose up and then were drawn away as the colors pulled them back like a retreating wave. In a few moments the colors faded and the jewel disappeared.

I looked down at Darryl. His face was peaceful. I could see that he had somehow turned old—very old—and that he was no longer alive. My eyes stung and I turned away.

Dad and I waited as the cops made their way down the 310 steps.

We rode back to San Francisco in the back of the police car. This time I didn't feel spooked, riding in the cage.

I wondered what the cops would put on their report. How could they describe such strange events? I guessed that it was something Dad and I could laugh about later.

As we got farther and farther from Point Reyes, I felt a mix of emotions. "I was the one," as Darryl had said. That made me feel good. I hadn't let him down—although I knew a lot of luck had been involved.

And how wrong I was about being an expert judge of people! Darryl, who I thought was going to be self-centered and sneaky, turned out to be a hero. And Dad, the guy I thought was a hopeless quitter, was slowly winning a hard-fought battle. I was proud to be his son. I leaned against his shoulder and went to sleep.

COMPREHENSION QUESTIONS

RECALL

1. What was Nick's first impression of Darryl's personality?

2. When they burst into Nick's room, who did the enemy aliens pretend to be?

3. In what strange way did Darryl eat his food?

ANALYZING CHARACTERS

1. What two words could describe Nick? Explain your thinking.
   •courageous •spiteful •faithful

2. What two words could describe Darryl? Explain your thinking.
   •boring •desperate •unusual

3. What two words describe Kara? Explain your thinking.
   •resourceful •ruthless •suspicious

4. What two words could describe Nick's dad? Explain your thinking.
   •critical •regretful •helpful

DRAWING CONCLUSIONS

1. What was in Darryl's briefcase?

2. Why did Kara think that Nick needed "serious help"?

3. What conclusion did Darryl draw about the tiny insect on the bus?

4. What did Darryl mean when he said that Nick was "safe"?

WHO AND WHERE?

1. Where were Darryl and Nick when Darryl first used his tube weapon?

2. Where were Nick and Darryl when the police started chasing them?

3. Who was a foreman at the printing plant?

4. Where was Darryl supposed to meet his spaceship?

VOCABULARY

1. The old lighthouse light had a thousand prisms. What is a *prism*?

2. Nick's dad rummaged through the glove compartment for a weapon. What are you doing when you *rummage*?